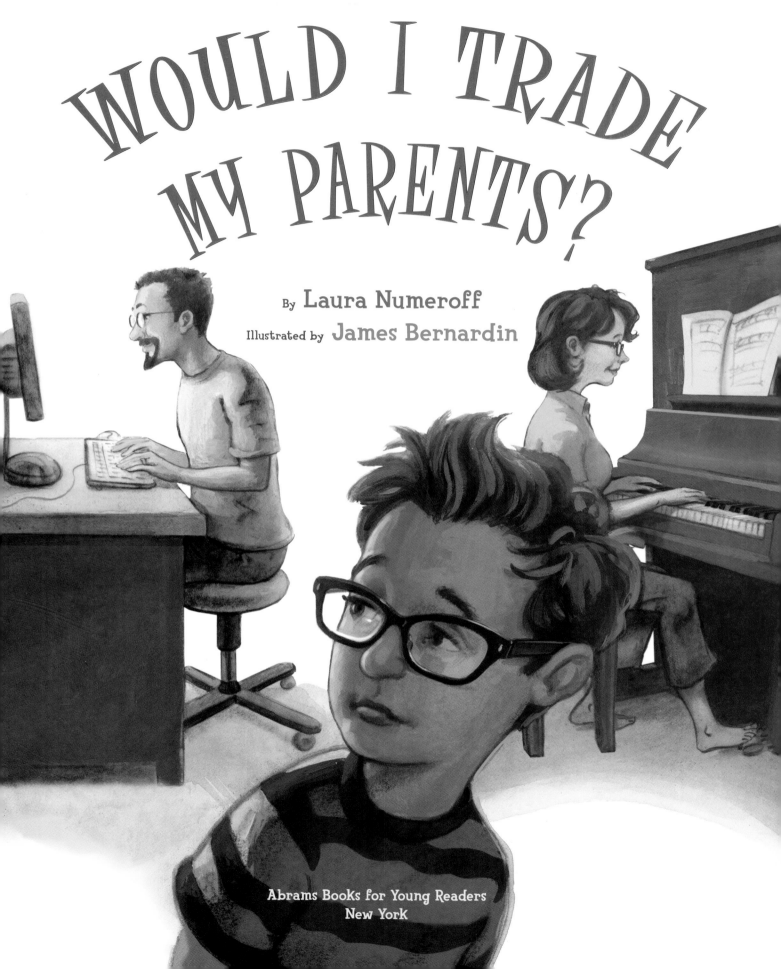

WOULD I TRADE MY PARENTS?

By Laura Numeroff

Illustrated by James Bernardin

Abrams Books for Young Readers
New York

The illustrations in this book were made with
acrylic paints and a digital paint program.

Library of Congress Cataloging-in-Publication Data

Numeroff, Laura Joffe.
Would I trade my parents? / by Laura Numeroff ;
illustrated by James Bernardin.
p. cm.
Summary: A young boy considers what is special about all of his friends' parents,
and realizes that his own are the most wonderful of all.
ISBN 978-0-8109-0637-2
[1. Parents–Fiction. 2. Individuality–Fiction.] I. Bernardin, James, ill. II. Title.
PZ7.N964Iaaw 2009
[E]–dc22
2008030381

Text copyright © 2009 Laura Numeroff
Illustrations copyright © 2009 James Bernardin

Book design by Chad W. Beckerman

Printed and bound in China
10 9 8 7 6 5 4 3 2 1

Abrams Books for Young Readers are available at special discounts when purchased in quantity for premiums and
promotions as well as fundraising or educational use. Special editions can also be created to specification.
For details, contact specialmarkets@hnabooks.com or the address below.

HNA ◼◼◼◼◼
harry n. abrams, inc.
a subsidiary of La Martinière Groupe
115 West 18th Street
New York, NY 10011
www.hnabooks.com

In memory of Florence and William Numeroff,
the best parents ever!
—L. N.

To my son Bryson, with thanks, for teaching me
the value of nonsense
—J. B.

Jason wouldn't trade his parents.

He thinks they're the best.

His dad builds houses.

He even built the house they live in.

It has lots of great places for hide-and-seek.

Jason's mom stays home and takes care of his twin sisters, Sarah and Lily.

She says it's the best job in the whole world.

His parents make blueberry pancakes for breakfast.

I wish my parents made blueberry pancakes for breakfast.

Katie wouldn't trade her parents.
She thinks they're the best.
Katie's mom is a dentist.

She drives a big old convertible.

Sometimes she takes us for a ride and puts the top down.

It's neat to look up at the sky!

Katie's father is an eye doctor.

He has a stamp collection.

Her parents let her watch TV until eight o'clock.

She just has to have her homework finished first.

I wish my parents let me watch TV until eight o'clock.

Ben wouldn't trade his parents.

He thinks they're the best.

His mom is an artist.

She painted a picture of Ben.

It looks just like him!

His dad is a photographer.

He went to Africa and took lots of pictures.

They even have one of a lion.

There are paintings and photographs all over the house.

Ben and his parents like to go camping.

I went with them once.

We slept under the stars!

I wish my parents let me sleep under the stars.

Sydney wouldn't trade her parents.

She thinks they're the best.

Her mom is taller than her dad.

She's a hairdresser.

Her hair always looks nice.

So does Sydney's.

Her dad is a plumber.

He fixed our sink when it leaked.

At night, her parents teach square dancing in their basement.

Sydney and I like to dance with them.

Once, we bumped into her father while we were dancing and couldn't stop giggling.

Sydney is allowed to have chocolate milk before dinner.

I wish my parents let me have chocolate milk before dinner.

William wouldn't trade his parents.

He thinks they're the best.

He lives with his mother but sees his father every weekend.

I asked if he missed having his dad around.

He said he does, but they have a great time when they're together.

He has his own bedroom in both of their houses!

His dad does something in an office, but I'm not sure what.

His mom owns a pet shop.

William has three cats, two hamsters, some fish, and a dog named Olive.

I wish my parents let me have a dog.

And then there are my parents . . .

My mother is a French teacher.

She taught me that "très bien" means "very good,"
and "merci" means "thank you."

Not only is she smart, but she also tells great jokes.

She can play the piano.

Sometimes we play duets!

Whenever I feel sad, she knows just
the right thing to say.

My dad is a writer.

He works at home in the den.

He writes books for grown-ups.

When I come home from school, we go for
a walk and talk about all kinds of things.

He knows a lot about nature.

He told me the names of all the different clouds.

My parents don't let me eat blueberry pancakes for breakfast like Jason.

Or watch TV until eight o'clock like Katie.

Or go camping like Ben.

Or drink chocolate milk before dinner like Sydney.

Or have pets like William.

But my mom puts a note in my lunch box every day.

And my dad reads to me every night.

And on weekends, we all go for a bicycle ride.

I wouldn't trade my parents.

I KNOW they're the best!